click
click
click!

For all the well-loved and well-worn toys in the family.
Blah Blah, Lizzie and Pengy, you know who you are!

This paperback edition first published in 2021 by Andersen Press Ltd.
First published in 2020 by Andersen Press Ltd.,
20 Vauxhall Bridge Road, London, SW1V 2SA, UK
Vijverlaan 48, 3062 HL Rotterdam, Nederland

Copyright © Julia Woolf 2020

Printed and bound in China.

1 3 5 7 9 10 8 6 4 2

British Cataloguing in Publication Data Available.

ISBN 978 1 78344 918 7

Julia Woolf

Duck & Penguin DO NOT Like Sleepovers

Andersen Press

This is Betty and Maud. They are best friends and they love spending time together. Especially with their favourite toys, Duck and Penguin.

Duck and Penguin aren't so keen on spending time together. Occasionally they can be nice to each other... but only occasionally.

Betty and Maud are beyond excited.
They are having a sleepover.

But not just any sleepover!
"We're going to spend the night together...

... in a TENT!"
squeals Betty.

"A teeny
weeny tiny
tent," says
Maud.

"So we'll be nice and cosy, staying together," says Betty.
"All... night... long!"

Duck and Penguin aren't so sure.

Betty and Maud
are going to camp
in the garden.
First they must
put up the tent.

"These pop-up tents are the best," says Betty.

"Yes they are," says Maud,

"just throw them
up in the air,
and..."

POP!

"Oh look! Penguin is flying with the tent!" says Betty.
"Ha ha ha, such a clever Penguin," says Maud.

With the pegs in, Betty and Maud
are checking the tent is secure.
"The ropes are nice and tight," says Betty.

"That's good," says Maud, "but be
careful not to trip over them."

"Oh yes," says Betty. "Otherwise
you could fall over."

Inside the tent, Betty and Maud are
getting things ready for bedtime.
"Oh, it's so cosy in here," says Betty.
"The sleeping bags are so
snuggly," says Maud.
"Duck and Penguin are going
to love these super-soft
pillows," says Betty.

While the girls have been inside the tent, outside it has started to get dark.

"Oooh," says Betty, "let's get our jammies on."

"Duck and Penguin love wearing their onesies," says Maud.

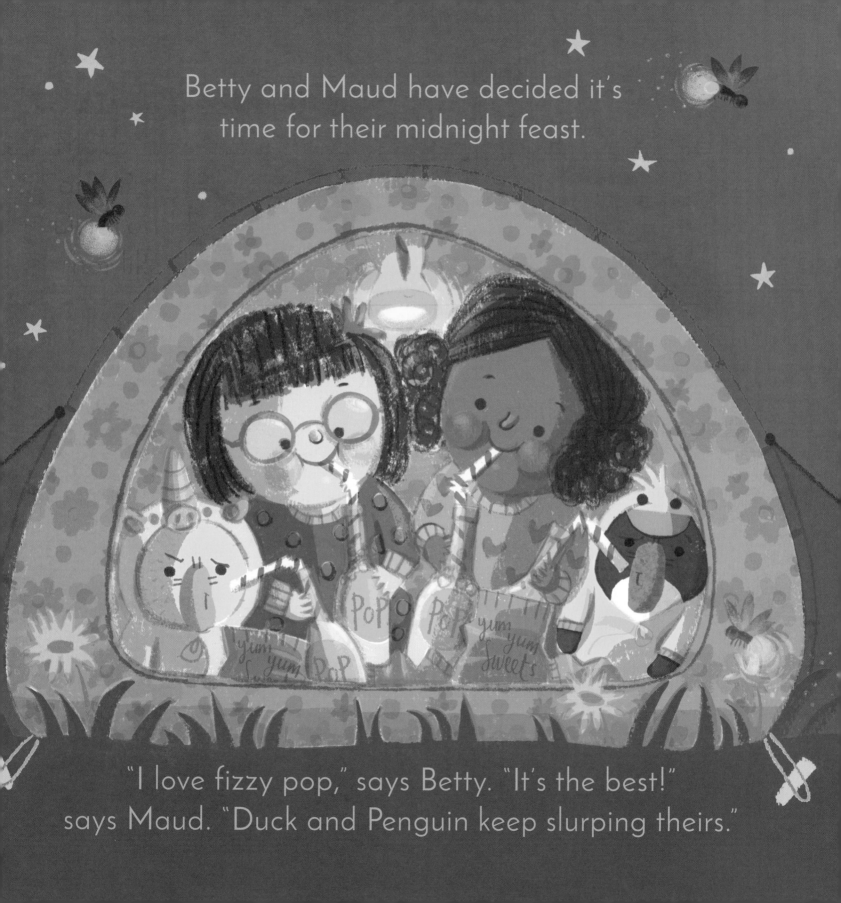

Betty and Maud have decided it's time for their midnight feast.

"I love fizzy pop," says Betty. "It's the best!" says Maud. "Duck and Penguin keep slurping theirs."

Oh dear, Betty and Maud have drunk too much fizzy pop! "I need a wee," says Betty. "Me too," says Maud, "I'm bursting."

"Let's go back to the house," says Betty.
"Quick!" says Maud.

And off they run.

Oh no, Betty and Maud have left Duck and Penguin behind. Duck and Penguin do not like sleepovers.

Duck and Penguin do not like being in the teeny weeny tiny tent.

Duck and Penguin have decided to go back to the house too.

Snort, shuffle

Skittle, scuttle

Outside there are lots of
strange noises.

Duck and Penguin are not that keen on all the strange noises.

Duck and Penguin aren't too sure where they are.

And they're having difficulty finding the house.

Duck and Penguin have the feeling...

that something is watching them.

Duck and Penguin think it might be a
good idea to get back to the tent.

Duck and Penguin like being in
the teeny weeny tiny tent.

The sun is up, and
after a good night's sleep, in a bed,
in the house, Betty and Maud have
come back to the tent to find
Duck and Penguin.

"Oh look," says Maud. "Kitty Kat has been looking after Duck and Penguin all night."

"I think Duck and Penguin must have
had the best night's sleep ever," says Betty.
"They really, really love sleepovers," says Maud.
"In the teeny weeny tiny tent," says Betty.

BURP!

POP

POP